a novella

HIT OR
MISTLETOE

h.j. harley

HIT
OR
MISTLETOE

A Novella

BY
HJ HARLEY

Please Note this is a work of fiction. Names, characters, places, and incidents either are the product of the author's imagination or are used fictitiously, and any resemblance to actual persons, living or dead, business establishments, events or locales is entirely coincidental.

Edited By Serena Clarke

Cover design by Sommer Stein of Perfect Pear

Dedication

For Heidi because she's awesome.

I'd only just dropped my books on the bed, and my roommate was knocking on my door. Love the girl and all, but her habit of not letting me get through the door before she was rattling shit off in that New Jersey accent was not going to be a selling point when she started looking for a new roommate next year. When I graduated in the spring, that was one thing I definitely would not miss.

"Hey, London. Trent called me." She swung on the molding of the door into my room, then fell back on my bed. My books bounced around, and one fell on the floor.

"Dammit, Lola. What did he want?" Clearly annoyed, I picked the book up off the floor.

"He was looking for you. Said he was worried because you haven't been answering your phone or his texts all day. I think it's sweet that your twin brother worries about you like that." She twirled a piece of hair around her finger mindlessly. "Do you two have that weird twin connection? Like if you were hurt he'd feel it too? He would know if you needed help or something, right?" she asked, staring at the ceiling. Another selling point…she's fucking weird, but in that 'it grows on you' sort of way.

"Not really. It's more like a bat signal. We shine our special lights in the northern sky and hope the other is just sitting around star-gazing to see it," I answered animatedly with a cheesy fake smile, then topped it off with the grand finale of resting bitch face.

"Jesus, you need some Dr. Phil in your life," she said as she sat up and leaned back on her elbows. "So how come you're ignoring Trent's calls?"

"I wasn't ignoring him, Lola. It's because this happened." I reached in my pocket, pulled out my shattered, dinged-up cell phone, and tossed it on her stomach.

"Holy shit, London, what the hell happened to your smart phone?" She held it up and gave a quick laugh as she examined it.

"It's a cell phone," I pointed out. I don't care if you can navigate the Kardashians to another planet with the damn thing…it's a cell phone. I refuse to call it a smart phone.

"Anyhow, you should call him back. He's worried." She stood and put the crushed phone on my desk next to my book, then handed me her own phone from her back pocket.

"Thanks." I smiled.

"No problem. You want brinner?" she asked. Brinner was when you had breakfast for dinner.

"Yes, brinner would be great."

"Yesss. Brinner bitches fo' life, yo." She pointed at me then slammed her fist on her chest twice with a mock sadness, before going out.

We'd had brinner a lot over the years. I'd definitely miss that. She was an amazing cook.

I picked up her phone and called Trent back.

He answered on the first ring. "Lola?"

"No, it's me."

"London. Where the hell have you been?" he asked, all pissyish. "I've been trying you all day."

"Hello sister. Hello brother. So nice of you to call me on this lovely day. I tried earlier, but alas, you did not answer…" I teased him with the mock conversation we should have had. "I have a life outside of answering your calls. I know it isn't the glamorous life of Trent Parker Skye, star center for UMD, but it's mine."

He ignored me and went right into the next question. "Why are you calling from Lola's phone?"

"I was leaving the lecture hall and dropped my phone while I was going down the steps. Someone stepped on it before I could pick it up. So, I'm using Lola's. Anything else? Did you have more questions about me and my whereabouts for your survey?" I laughed.

"I'll be there at nine a.m. London. Nine. Please don't make us late. There's a storm coming in and I want to make it back home before it hits. My two front tires need replacing. Oh and pack light, last minute change of plans. I have a friend coming along. He'd be spending the holidays here at school otherwise, so I invited him."

"Does Mom know?" I asked with a bit of caution.

"Yes, London, Mom knows," he said with a mischievous snicker.

"Trent, I'm not giving up my bed," I told him.

He gave a chuckle. "Of course not, Princess."

"Trent, I'm dead serious. Don't bring home any more head cases – like Hannah, who thought she and I were BFFs just because you two were doing it. Bitch took over my room, puked in my bed, and borrowed my favorite sweatshirt…then she mailed it back in five hundred pieces because *you* broke up with her. And don't even get me started about when she knocked over Grandma's ashes and blamed Tuna…"

"Don't worry London, I'm not. See you in the a.m." He hung up.

As I went to go give Lola her phone back, I got a whiff of waffles and heard Beyoncé blasting from the kitchen. She was singing and pouring the waffle batter into the maker when she noticed me.

"Turn that down." She nodded her head back in the direction of the iPod dock. I did as she asked, then put her phone on the counter.

"Thanks for the phone." I hopped up on the stool and sat on the opposite side of where she was cooking.

"All good?" She closed the waffle maker, and wiped her hands on the towel.

"Eh," I muttered, less than enthusiastic, my face leaned against my hand and my cheek mushed up into my eye. "He'll be here at nine, and I have to pack light because he's bringing a friend home."

Lola's eyes widened, and she smiled. *Oh no. Here it comes.*

"A hot friend?"

Yep, nosy, nosy. "Oh, yeah, for sure." I sat up straight and smiled. "My brother said he's an absolute dreamboat." I rolled my eyes and laughed, and Lola joined me.

"I can't even with you. Dreamboat? London, you're a mess." She turned her attention back to the waffle maker. She knew I wouldn't be talking men with her. I never talked about dating or guys or anything to do with romance – I couldn't afford any distractions. Trent was getting a full ride on a hockey scholarship at the University of Minnesota, Duluth. I was going to the University of Minnesota, St. Paul, and I had no such luck in the scholarship department. The thing about Minnesota is, everyone is smart. Like smart, smart. So, unlike so many other places, you needed a sport to get you a scholarship, because being exceptional academically didn't cut it. You needed to one-up 'em – brains *and* a talent. So I'd be buried in schoolwork for the next four years, at least. My parents could've helped out, especially with Trent having a free ride, but after my mom's second bout with breast cancer two years ago, it left the money tree a bit bare. And nobody would be going broke on my account. I survived on ramen noodles and the condiment bar down at the cafeteria. They had a mean mustard packet, that's for sure. I knew I'd be okay though – my parents wouldn't allow me to starve.

"Honestly, though, it's your last year...why not be a Ho Ho Ho this holiday season? Maybe Deck a Ball or two." She winked and blew me a kiss seductively, and I threw the roll of duct tape that was sitting in front of me at her.

"Oh yeah. Can't wait. What's worse than obnoxious frat guys? Obnoxious hockey players, that's what."

"But at least the frat guys have all their teeth," she joked.

"So you say," I laughed. "Besides, having sex in my parents' house isn't really on my list of top ten things to do in my lifetime."

"You are such a prude." She handed me my plate.

"I'm not a prude. I just have standards, and belching the alphabet forward and backwards in less than a minute is not one of them. That's if they even know their ABCs." I began eating.

"You are such a bitch, London," she joked as she sat down to eat too.

"Sticks and stones Lola, sticks and stones. I've never done the walk of shame. Can you say the same?" I eyed her suspiciously.

"We're talking about you here, don't drag me into it. I can see it now. You're going to be that weird old neighborhood lady who hoards birds, just watch." She said between bites.

"Hoarding birds? I always figured I'd be the old ferret lady who stinks like pee."

"Nice, keeping your options open. Good thinking. Look, go let someone knock the dust out of there for you. It's got to suck always cleaning your own house." She snickered.

Lola 1, London 0

"There's something wrong with your brain." I shook my head and smiled at her.

In all honesty, sometimes I felt as if I'd always be too busy for a relationship. I've always had a reason not to get into one. I was in middle school when my mom was diagnosed with breast cancer, so I spent most of my free time with her, either at chemo or at home. Trent didn't spend as much time at home as I did. I think it was harder on him and my dad because they felt helpless. Like, they were men, they should have been able to protect her from all the bad shit that was happening, and they couldn't. So keeping busy was an essential defense mechanism. My dad was around a lot more than Trent, but even so he spent a lot of time in the barn and stuff. He never missed a single doctor's appointment or radiation therapy session though. The chemo he didn't handle so well, because it was in a dialysis clinic, which reminded him too much of my grandma Skye who'd passed a few years earlier from kidney failure.

Then in high school I was too busy remaking friends to worry about a boyfriend. I had one or two here and there, but nothing too serious. Trent says it's because I have impossible standards – that's why he's called me Princess most of my life. I beg to differ. I think he just has incredibly *low* standards.

But then in our junior year Mom came out of remission, and it started all over. I missed my junior and senior proms – according to Trent I didn't miss much, but I never believed him. My mom always begged me to go out, even if it meant tagging along with Trent and his buddies. I didn't want to go, though. I didn't know how much longer I'd have her around, so I wanted to be with her every minute I could.

By the time remission rolled around for the second time, it was the summer of my freshman year in college. I knew I'd have to bust my butt, so once again…no time. The more I thought about it, the more they sounded like excuses instead of reasons. Either way, I'd just never had a long-term relationship.

I was fine with that.

Most of the time, anyway.

Chapter 2

I woke up at seven-thirty, and was showered, makeup on, hair straightened and ready by eight forty-five. *Ha! Take that, Trent.* I finished packing up the last of my essentials and headed to the living room to wait on him.

I called out to Lola but she didn't answer. When I knocked on her bedroom door, she grumbled very loudly to come in.

"Hey, I'm leaving," I informed her.

"Okay, bye. Be safe. Go get laid or something." She rolled over and punched her pillow to her liking.

"You're so stupid." I laughed at her response. "You sure you don't want to come along? Who knows, maybe you and the dreamboat will hit it off," I snickered. She hauled a smaller pillow at me and said something unintelligible. I laughed again and picked the pillow up, and tossed it back on her bed.

She turned over onto her side and faced me. "No, thanks. I'm going to my dad's. He convinced me."

"You mean he bribed you…" I grinned.

"Bribed, convinced. Same thing. Don't judge me." She closed her eyes and yawned.

I heard the horn honk. "He's early."

"Good. Go. Goodbye. Have a great Christmas or whatever it is you Eskimos do up there in Northern Minnesota." She smirked and pulled the covers over her head.

"Bye, Lola. Merry Christmas." I went over and hugged her, and she hugged me back through the blanket.

"Text me when you get your phone fixed so I can harass you with pictures of my ugly-ass step-dog. Fucking Maltipoo-poo." She faded out as I walked away laughing. She was a trip. At that moment, I regretted not inviting her sooner. There's no way Trent's houseguest would be more of a good time than Lola. We always had laughs.

Trent was knocking as I opened the front door.

"Ready?" he asked hurriedly. "Storm's moving faster than expected. We can *not* get stuck in this shit." He took the two bags from my hands and headed back to his truck.

After I locked up I stood for a moment trying to see if I knew who was in the front seat. I knew most of Trent's buddies, especially the hockey players, because I went to a lot of his games. But all I could make out was a red hat, because of the glare on the windows.

"You two have enough shit in there? This is why I had to pack light?" I called out to him when I walked to the truck and saw the back part crammed with crap.

"Just get in, London." He slammed the back door down and walked around to the driver's side.

"And why is he in the front seat? You know I get car sick," I said as I approached the passenger side. I knocked on the window and he rolled it down.

"Lon-donnnnn." Red hat guy catcalled my name, followed by a whistle. "Look at you."

Aw, crap...not him. Anyone but him...

"Hi, Pratt. I get car sick, get in the back." I tried to yank the door open.

"No can do." He slapped his hand on the lock before I could get it open, then followed it with a wink.

"Oh my God. Trent!" I shouted through the open window. "Are you serious with this shit? Of all people, you bring *this guy* home for Christmas? There wasn't a criminal or a hitchhiker available instead?"

Pratt just sat there with a playful smug grin on his face, and turned his hat backwards.

"London," Trent said. "Get in. You stopped getting car sick when you were eight." He put the truck in drive and waited.

"Twelve, you asshole. You're my brother, you're supposed to be on my side," I said as I opened the back door.

"Trust me, I am on your side. We had Taco Bell for breakfast," Trent informed me, and let out a belch. "Oh, man. Excuse me. That one slipped out." He banged on his chest lightly.

"You are so gross," I scoffed.

"Because Princess London doesn't do bodily functions, I forgot," Trent teased me, then both he and Pratt laughed.

"I hate you. I hope I throw up on you." I went to go sit in the back in the seat, but Pratt stepped out of the passenger side.

"You have such a sunny disposition, London." He gave me a wink, and I rolled my eyes, but I felt a bit guilty for being bitchy.

"Thanks for the front seat, Eighty-Six," I said.

Pratt Montgomery. Number eight-six. My brother's right-hand man – well, his right wing man on the team. He's what they call a 'power forward'. He has both the physical size and the offensive skills to pretty much do it all – the 'complete' hockey player package. He's been tugging on my ponytails since our freshman year of college, talking a lot of harmless flattering and sometimes annoying smack, but he's never been disrespectful or taken it too far. If he had, my brother would've taken his kneecaps out with a hockey stick.

I woke to Pratt's big-ass head in my face – I must have dozed off at some point. He was stretched out between the seats, nearly hovering over me.

"Wakey, wakey. We're almost home."

I turned my head. "Your breath smells like a donkey's ass."

"You know what donkey's ass smells like why, again?" He sat back in his seat.

"And it's our home, not yours," I snapped. "Don't you have your own family to torture during the holidays?"

"London. Christ, be nice." My brother gave me a wide-eyed look in the rearview mirror, and then turned into our driveway. We lived about a quarter mile off the road.

"Nah, it's cool bro. I can handle a little London attitude." Pratt said, but not in his normal fun, challenging tone. It seemed like a forced statement.

Whoops, I must have struck a nerve. Never took him for a sensitive one. I guess I'll try and be less excessive in the bitch department. Besides, his breath was nowhere near a donkey's ass. It was actually very minty.

As we approached the house I could see my mom in the kitchen through the window. I couldn't wait to hug her. When we stopped in the driveway my chocolate lab, Tuna, hopped up at the storm door, pushed down on the handle to open it, and came running out of the house. I could officially begin my last Christmas vacation from school. I couldn't wait to hug my parents and have Tuna jump up and knock me over. Labs were known for their clumsy tails, but Tuna's would wag uncontrollably at his first sight of me, and Mom's plants were collateral damage. You'd think she'd just move the damn things.

I hopped out of the truck when we came to a stop, and right on cue Tuna jumped up, knocking me off balance. I slammed into Pratt, who'd just gotten out too, and he caught me. *Jesus, he barely moved when I fell into him.* I quickly straightened myself out and gave him a light shove away.

"I got it, thanks," I said as I bent down to pet Tuna.

"Any time, gorgeous. Especially if you keep bending over like that," Pratt teased as he walked around to the back of the truck.

I couldn't help but smile, without him seeing of course. It's always nice when someone pays you a compliment. By that time I for sure felt terrible about behaving like a jerk. He didn't really deserve the over-exaggeration about his breath, either. But judging by his comment, it seemed like he'd gotten over it – if he'd even been bothered in the first place. I laughed to myself.

My mom came out of the house, cursing at Tuna over the path of destruction he'd left.

"Tuna, I'm going to put a damn cone around your tail until you learn how to stop taking out everything in your way. Like a brown drooling tornado, I tell you." She gave me a hug, then pulled back to look at me. "Hey sweetie. How was the ride?"

"The ride sucked." I always laid it on thick with my mom. But now I studied her for a moment to see how *she* was doing. She looked great. She had color in her cheeks and they were a little bit fuller since the last time I saw her. Which was good, because that meant she still had a good appetite and was gaining weight. All great signs everything was going well health-wise.

"Oh, I'm sure you're fine. You stopped getting car sick when you were eight. And stop trying to analyze me London. I'm feeling fine." She rubbed my arm then began to walk over to my brother and Pratt.

"Twelve, and what the what? You knew?" I gave a short laugh.

"Your brother told me," she admitted.

"Trent, you a-hole," I said to him as I followed Mom towards the back of the truck to get my bags.

"She sat in the front anyhow, Mrs. S. Don't let her make me out to be ungentlemanly like." Pratt had on his best smile. *Ew. He has nice teeth. Dammit.*

"Pratt, call me Linda, please," she said as she gave my brother a hug.

Pratt and I both reached for my bags.

"I got it, thanks." I swatted his hand away.

"No, please, your highness, allow me." There was that sneaky sarcastic grin. I had to hold back my own while I took a step back and motioned with my arm, allowing him to take them out.

He smiled a big cheesy smile as if he was proud of himself, and pulled my bags out for me.

"Thanks," I mumbled.

"Get over here, Eighty-Six. How are you doing, sweetheart?" I heard my mom say as I walked towards the door with Tuna in tow.

"Sweetheart? Wow, Mom, you're really reaching there a bit aren't you?" I said as I reached the porch and headed inside.

"London, be nice," I heard her say from not too far behind me.

"Dad?" I called out. I didn't see his truck outside, but sometimes he left it out back with the plow on it before storms, so it was easier to get out.

"He isn't back from your aunt's yet," Mom said. "Ever since she slipped down the steps, he makes sure to pre-treat her driveway and front porch before a storm hits."

"Mom, do you want to take a ride with me to get a replacement phone before it starts to get too bad out there? I dropped mine in the lecture hall, and it got trampled." I pulled it from my pocket and shook it back and forth in my hand to show her.

"Sure, but we'll have to go right now."

"Okay. Just let me bring this stuff upstairs and use the bathroom." I gave her a quick kiss on the cheek, and ran up to my room with my bags.

When I got back downstairs Trent told me Mom was in the car waiting for me. As I approached the car, the only thing I could see was the red hat in the window.

"Mother effer," I shouted. As I got closer I could see his big-toothed, aggravating smile, and my mom was laughing too.

"Eighty-Six." I opened the door and whined while I tugged unsuccessfully on his jacket. The big fathead didn't even budge.

I let out a frustrated 'errrrrrgggggggg' and slammed the door while my mom and Eighty-Six had a good laugh at my expense.

"Oh, London, be courteous. He wouldn't be very comfortable back there. It's not roomy like Trent's truck," she said in Pratt's defense.

"Oh my God, what is wrong with you people? You call yourself family? Bunch of traitors." I plopped in the back seat, and slammed my own door to make my point.

"Oh damn, I forgot my wallet. I'll be right back," Mom said, halfway out of the car already.

While she was gone, we sat in silence. I liked it that way. I was still aggravated at that massive melon-head in the front seat.

Next thing I saw was Tuna bolting out the front door and running straight for the woods. I jumped out to grab him before he got too far off looking for my brother or dad. When I bent over to pet him, I heard a whistle from behind me.

"Dear sweet *Jesus* on a Huffy, London. I like those jeans on you," Pratt said.

"Way to woo a woman, Eighty-Six," I responded.

"You know what else I like on you, London?" he asked with slightly puckered lips and a head nod.

"Really? Let me guess…'You'. That's what else you like on me," I scoffed.

"Woooahhh, slow down tiger, I'm not that kind of guy. I was going to say I like all that sass you got on you, but hey, if you wanna go there, I'll give it a try. Just be gentle." He gave me a doe-eyed stare and batted his eyelashes.

I couldn't help but laugh. "You are such an idiot."

I sent Tuna back in the house and my mom held the door open for him, then we both got back in the car, ready to go.

"Wait. Stop," Pratt said.

"What now?" I asked, annoyed.

"Does anyone need to use the potty before we leave?" he asked.

"I can't. Just stop talking. You're like this weird man-child." I pulled my iPod out and put my ear buds in, with a cheeky smile on my face.

He just turned around and gave me that irritating grin. But this time, I noticed he had a dimple on one side, and his eyes were gray like the sky. They contrasted with his black shaggy hair that had a bit of a curl at the ends.

Eighty-Six 1, London 0

Chapter 3

While I picked out my replacement phone, Eighty-Six teased me the entire time. I must have called him every other name in the book, and probably made up a few words, too. After we were finished there, my mom had to get some groceries. She had an irrational fear of running out of food. We were so stocked up we'd qualify to be on an episode of Hoarders: Snowstorm Edition.

While Mom and I walked around the store, I messed around with my new phone. Thank God it was a cakewalk transferring everything over to it – I haven't remembered a phone number since 2003. Pratt had gone across the street to get some coffee. I was surprised when he asked if I wanted something. I graciously declined, which I'm sure surprised him too. *Look at us, full of surprises, Mr. Montgomery.*

The heat must have been jacked up to 100 degrees in the grocery store, and I was getting really hot, so I told Mom I'd wait outside for her. When I left the store, there was one of those kid horsey rides – the kind you put a quarter in and it gives you whiplash. I sat on it sideways and unzipped my jacket, concentrating on my phone. Suddenly the damn horse started bucking around, and I nearly fell off. Pratt had stuck a quarter in it while I wasn't paying attention.

"Dammit, Eighty-Six." I tried to get off, but he blocked me.

"Nope, I'm taking you on a ride."

I had to laugh at the mischievous look on his face. It was cute, I couldn't resist.

"You're such a clown, Pratt."

I remained sidesaddle on this tiny bucking horse until it stopped. When it finally did, I went to get off and my foot slipped. I was headed face first into the pavement. The whole thing was playing out in slow motion…I was going to be in a full body cast with my face mangled by the concrete, and my new phone would be a paperweight. Instinctively, I put my hands out to break my fall, but Pratt caught me.

He lifted me so I was on my feet, even with his shoulders. "That's twice I've saved your pretty little ass, London."

"Thank you. You saved my phone too."

"Yep, you should thank me later." He wiggled his eyebrows up and down. His black curls stuck out from under his hat, and I found myself wanting to touch them. *All right London, don't be weird.*

"I'll send you a card." I rolled my eyes and turned my back to him, but I was smiling.

"Look what I got while I was waiting on my coffee," he said.

I turned back around to look, and there was something clipped to his hat, hanging in his face. *Mistletoe.*

"You are such a child," I scoffed playfully. "What, are you planning to carry that around hoping to score with random women?"

"Admit it. You wanna kiiiiissss me." He puckered up his lips like a fish.

"Grow up, Eighty-Six. And not if you were the last set of lips on this planet." I laughed and smacked his arm.

Then I heard my mom's voice from behind. "You kids ready?"

"Sure am. Shotgun!" I called, as I dodged around Pratt to follow her back to the car.

"Shotgun." He mimicked, then jumped in front of me when we got to the car. He picked me up from under my arms and moved me aside like a cardboard cut-out. I was sort of impressed by just how strong he was. But I was not impressed with my lack of resistance to how he made me feel when he touched me. Even just goofing around, he made my heart race and my skin get hot. I could feel the heat rise in my cheeks every time. *Not good.*

"Seriously, you have no manners. What happened to ladies first?" I asked with my hands on my hips.

"Just keepin' it real, London. This way, when you fall in love with me it's all out there." He opened the front passenger side door for me, and I eyed him up and down before getting in.

"Never gonna happen, bub." I shook my head and gave a small laugh. I had to admit, if nothing else, he was cute and entertaining.

When we rolled up back at the house, I was happy to see my dad's truck in the driveway. I went around to the trunk to help with the groceries, but Pratt had beaten me to it.

"Just close the trunk," he said.

"Just close the trunk what, Pratt? How do we ask for things? See...man-child," I scoffed.

"Now?" he responded, trying to hold back a smile.

I shut the trunk when I heard my mom yelling at Tuna as he ran out the door. We both laughed and headed towards the house.

As soon as I walked in I saw my dad and Trent round the corner, and my dad's face lit up. They both had grease on their clothes – they must have been in the barn making sure all the equipment was tuned up and working properly.

"There's my girl," he said, walking to me with open arms.

"Hi, Daddy. I missed you." I hugged him tight, not caring about the grease. *I was a Daddy's girl…don't judge me.*

"How you doing, kiddo?" he asked, as he looked me over.

"I'm great. The mess hall condiment bar feeds me well," I joked.

He chuckled. "Oh yeah?"

"Yep, all-you-can-eat mustard packets fit for a princess," I said as I took off my jacket. I hung it up on the hook as Pratt set the bags on the kitchen table.

"Ohhhhhh, look who it is. Eighty-Six! Come on over here boy, give me a bro hug," my dad shouted with enthusiasm.

"A bro hug?" Trent and I mouthed to each other with expressions of horror crossed with confusion, then laughed.

"Hey, Mr. Skye. How are you?" Pratt said as he 'bro hugged' my dad.

"Call me Will, Pratt. I hear enough Mr. Skye at work."

I left them to their conversation, and started helping my mom put up the groceries. With all the movement and opening and closing of the cabinets, I couldn't hear what was being said. I was bent over in front of the fridge when someone bumped into me from behind – and then I heard a snort. Pratt.

"You can be so immature," I said as I found a space for the ketchup. "No wonder you aren't with your family…they'd probably rather die than deal with you for the holidays."

I closed the fridge door and turned around to see my mom, dad and brother with jaws dropped, and Pratt with his hands in his pockets, looking up at the ceiling.

"What?" I asked.

Nobody responded. Just blank faces.

"What's with the faces?" I tried again.

"London. We raised you better than that. I'm so sorry, Pratt." My mom put her hand on his shoulder and rubbed it.

"What? He can handle an insult or two," I said in my own defense. "He's a big boy."

"No, it's cool Mrs. Skye," Pratt said. "No need to apologize. I actually need to make a phone call. Excuse me." He walked out the front door. Tuna even gave me a look of disappointment before he turned and headed out right behind him.

"Wait up, bro, I'm coming." Trent grabbed his jacket. "Really, London? Really? We all know you live in your own little world where you don't give a shit about anything but your grades and your future, but could you be any more of an insensitive bitch to him? Seriously." He shook his head and headed out the door after Pratt.

At that point I was so confused, and getting really annoyed. I folded my arms. "What the hell? How did I somehow end up the bad guy here?"

My parents looked at one another, and then back at me.

"She doesn't know, Will." Mom took a step towards me. "You don't know, do you London?"

"Know what? This is beyond frustrating."

"London, his family died in a car accident just over a year ago. It was snowing, a semi didn't stop in time, and his mom, dad, younger brother and sister were all killed. They were on the way to a charity hockey game Pratt was playing with the Minnesota Wild. You don't remember hearing about it?" Mom asked, still looking shocked.

"Oh no. No, no, no. That was *his* family? I remember something about it, but it was right around the time I was buried in research for my dissertation. Holy shit, Mom. I'm a complete and utter asshole." My heart sank, and I could feel that sting in my nose before my face exploded into tears. I went to the bathroom to wash my face real quick, then came back and grabbed my jacket.

"I gotta go talk to him," I said, with a bit more composure. I truly felt horrible. Didn't matter if I knew or not…I shouldn't have said that to him.

As I stepped outside, the snow was really coming down. I called for the guys but got no answer, so I walked towards the barn on the back side of the house, and saw the light on up in the loft. Our barn wasn't for animals, except some barn cats. We used it mostly as a safe, dry place to put all the equipment and other stuff we had. I had made the loft into a hang-out spot around my fifteenth birthday. That was my parents' present to me – my own space away to hang out, read, whatever I felt like. I strung white lights all over, and my mom and I had made a huge pillow bed on the floor. I loved it because it was my space, and my parents liked it because they could always see what was happening up there as soon as they walked in. Win win.

As I approached the barn, Trent came walking around from the side. I assumed he'd used 'nature's bathroom', because he was adjusting his belt.

"Good job, jackass," he called out to me.

"Yeah, I know, I feel terrible. I'm going to go talk to him," I answered, with my hand on the barn door handle.

"Well, just remember it isn't always about you and how you feel. Apologize and leave it at that. Don't do the whole 'I feel so bad' shit. He doesn't need pity, and he doesn't give a rat's ass about how you feel," Trent said, making it quite clear he thought I was a jerk.

"I'll keep it to a minimum," I shot back at him.

When he walked off, I took a deep breath and slid the oversized barn door open. It sounded like an old wooden rollercoaster as it slid across the track.

"Pratt?" I called out as I closed the door. "Can I talk to you?"

"Not now, London. I'm really not in the mood." I followed the sound of his voice up to the loft, and saw him sitting on the rafters looking out the small window at the top of the peak.

I climbed the ladder to the loft. "I'm a big, fat, insensitive, self-centered jerk, does that help?"

By the time I reached the top and stood up, he still hadn't answered me.

"I'm so sorry, Pratt. I didn't realize," I said. Then I turned and stepped back on the ladder to go down.

"Wait," he said, and I looked up to see him standing above me. "I'll forgive you on one condition."

He stood looking at me, and in that moment I saw the sadness in his eyes. *London…you are an idiot.* My stomach gave an angsty roll. He was actually very handsome when he wasn't being a meathead.

"What's that?" I asked.

He gave a crooked smile. "Admit it."

"Admit what?" I was clearly confused.

"Admit that you just wanna kiss me." He clipped the mistletoe to his hat again.

Yup. Meathead. I couldn't help but smile. On top of handsome, he was a real charmer when he wanted to be.

This could be trouble.

Then again, maybe that was just what I needed.

Chapter 4

We sat up in the loft until dusk. My mom checked in now and again to make sure we weren't cold or hungry. That was her story, at least, and she was sticking to it. She knew the barn was fully heated and insulated. Trent made some coffee and brought it up to us, and hung out for an hour or so. We talked hockey, school, and about my brother's psychotic ex-girlfriend, Hannah. That chick was one hell of a train wreck. Talk about trust issues. I have no idea who did what to her in life but damn, Trent paid for it the year they were together…and the year after that she spent stalking him.

My parents came up with dinner for us all while we were mid-conversation about her.

"Hey, remember at the Championship game in St. Paul you almost got into it with her, London?" Trent asked as he took a bite of his pizza.

"That was fun times," I answered with a mouthful.

"I remember you decided an aerial attack would be a good strategy," my father chimed in.

"Whatever. It wasn't an aerial attack – I jumped on her from two rows above. What was I supposed to do? She was about to throw a bottle over the glass at Trent." I defended my actions as I wiped my hands, and everyone laughed.

"That was the first time I ever had to break up a fight in the stands at a hockey game," Pratt said. "You get pretty strong when you're pissed."

"You were in there? I don't remember."

"I was." He looked at me and gave a small smile.

"It took me a second to register that it was you involved, London," Trent said. "That was way out of character for you. Once I saw Pratt had a hold of you I had to use my hockey stick to pull Hannah away. She tried hitting me with that bottle again once I released her."

"Well, it wasn't like I was shanking her in the stands or throwing punches, I was trying to get the *glass bottle* away from her. Besides, we'll always have that memory as one of the most exciting family outings ever."

I looked at Pratt when I said it. His lips tightened into a thin line and curled slightly at the corners, then he gave a little nod.

Did we just have a moment? I think we just had a moment.

We all laughed at the memory, and talked some more while we finished up dinner. I threw a piece of crust over the side to Tuna because he looked so pathetic down on the ground floor all alone. Then I helped Mom clean up, and we headed back to the house.

It was nearly six o'clock and the snow was still coming down pretty heavy. I watched Pratt play with Tuna in the snow, then went inside. The guys ended up staying outside to snow blow and salt the driveway and porch. I heard the snowmobile start up, and looked out the window to see my dad come around with the plow attached. Then I saw Pratt come up on the porch, sweeping away the last of the snow that had drifted in.

He turned to pick up the container of salt, and saw me watching him. When we made eye contact, my stomach felt like bingo balls were flying around in there. He winked and began salting. He had on a brown and mustard colored flannel and his hat was turned backwards. As I watched him work, I could see his muscles straining against the sleeves at times. His back was to me so I had a clear view of him from behind. I was looking at Eighty-Six in an entirely new light. He wasn't the typical jock college guy I'd convinced myself he was before I'd even gotten to know him. He was sort of sweet and charming, and he had a fun side too.

Damn, Lola would be proud of me.

We stayed snowed in for the next few days. We had plenty of food and nowhere to be, so we all just hunkered down. We watched TV, played cards and board games…you know, all that hokey fun shit you'd do as a kid, except now we could drink wine while we played UNO and Jenga. I went out and rode my snowmobile, and played with Tuna in the snow. I loved the snow. I loved the cold. I loved everything about the holidays.

One afternoon, Trent and Pratt joined me. Pratt was betting he could hang onto the tube attached to the back of my snowbie longer than me. He didn't know who he was messing with – I was the reigning champ in the family. Seven minutes, fourteen seconds I'd hung on to that bad boy, as my brother attempted to sidewind and shake me off in multiple directions. We had a trophy and everything. Well, not so much a trophy as one of those blow-up pool tubes. Whatever, it was mine. And there was no way in hell I was letting Pratt take the title from me.

"Alright, smart-ass. You think you can beat me? Trent…hook him up."

"Fine by me, Princess," Pratt shot back. "You'll never shake me – I'm too strong, and you're not an aggressive enough driver. Remember, I've seen you in action." He wiggled his eyebrows and grinned.

"You wish," I went back at him, and laughed. I changed my gloves as Trent made sure the tube was properly inflated and the back bumper cover was secure, just in case I stopped and Pratt slid into it.

My mom and dad joined us. I believe I heard my father say he was going to enjoy seeing the record being broken. Mom cheered me on, while Tuna was just being Tuna, barking and playing in the snow.

"Ready Eighty-Six?" I taunted him, as I took a seat on the snowbie.

"Bring it on, prissy-pants," he answered with a smirk.

"Oh, don't you worry. You'll be begging me for mercy by the time I'm finished with you." I cracked my knuckles in a cheesy fake attempt to be tough.

He bent over just close enough that I could feel the heat of his breath against my ear, and spoke in a deep, even, sexy-as-hell tone. "Don't tease me, London."

Oh shit...Eighty-Six has game. Damn. An odd feeling – angst, I suppose – ran through my veins, eventually reaching my cheeks and making them heat up. He smiled his irritatingly adorable dimple smile as he walked backwards towards the tube...never taking his eyes off of me.

I snapped out of whatever the fuck had just happened to me, and jumped and kick-started the snowbie. I pulled my goggles over my eyes and then revved the engine good a few times. I looked back at Pratt to see him sprawled on top of the tube with a hold on each handle.

Amateur. He won't last two minutes that way.

I waited in anticipation for the 'ready' signal. I couldn't wait to dump his ass on turn three. Not an aggressive driver? He had *no* idea that not only am I a tubing champ, but I'm also a certified Search and Rescuer for the local Mountie chapter. When people get stuck cross-country skiing, or hurt while coming down the mountain, I go up to help retrieve them. You have to be a skilled driver for that – one mistake on an incline or descent, and you'd be fucked seven ways to Sunday.

Pratt gave the signal, and I popped it into first and took off. Tuna chased us down the driveway until we approached the edge of the woods. I cut a hard right about fifty feet from the tree line, so that he seemed to be heading straight into a tree, but I knew he'd swing out and get pulled back in just shy of a trunk or two. I heard him shout and I laughed, never looking back. Once the barn was in sight, I turned right again – a bit easier, so he wouldn't hit the snow-covered fire pit – then I zig-zagged him back and forth, headed to the back of the house around the barn. When I hit the barn I cut a sharp left and sent him out wide to his right, nearly clipping my dad's vintage '62 Chevy. *Oops, that's a tetanus shot waiting to happen.* Then I glanced down at the timer on my dash. Three minutes so far.

I had to step it up, so I took him around the barn again, cutting back towards the clearing by the house and over the small snow pile that lined the path out to the barn and shed. I hit it full throttle again, to make sure I had enough speed for us both to clear it safely, and hit the jump. As the snowbie's front end went up, I heard Pratt yell something, and I slowed down to give him ample time to land. I didn't want to yank the tube out from under him and have his arms go with it, leaving his body behind. When he hit the ground he bounced once, twice, three times, then rolled off the tube into another snow pile.

I stood up, turned back around and flipped on the high beam so I could see him. His nose was bleeding. *Ahhh, fuck.*

"You okay?" I shouted. I cut the engine and hopped off, grabbing the first aid kit I kept in my seat compartment. He rolled onto his back, holding his face, and without even thinking I went into action. There was a pile of snow on one side, so I was lacking space to work on him. I put down my kit and scooped up a handful of snow, before straddling him.

"Let me see, Eighty-Six." I tugged at his hands in an attempt to pull them away from his face, and put the packed snow on his nose. I could see the blood dripping down his cheeks from both sides, and a small cut over his right eye. That was the least of my worries at that point. I could hear my brother calling from a distance, and my mother telling my father to go get a towel and a blanket.

"He busted his face, he isn't giving birth, Mom," I muttered under my breath, but I guess loud enough for Pratt to hear me, because he laughed.

"Well that's a good sign – you're responsive. Did you hit your head, or just your face?" I asked him as I took off my jacket and put it under his head.

"Both," he responded.

While I took out what I needed from the kit, I began asking him the routine questions you should always ask when it comes to head trauma.

"What's your name?"

"Pratt Montgomery."

"How old are you?" I cracked the icepack and shook it up to get cold.

"Twenty-three…and a half."

"Where are you?" I brushed what was left of the slushy snow from his nose and placed the ice pack over it.

"Heaven." He smiled, even with the blood running across his face. I rolled my eyes and placed rolled gauze under the ice pack, and told him to pinch the bridge if he could for a second.

"What's today's date?"

"I don't know, but when I find out it's going down as the best day of my life." He grinned again.

"Alright, I think you're as fine as you're going to get in the head department." I chuckled and stood up.

"Dude, you ate shit. You okay?" Trent reached us, laughing.

Pratt sat up on one elbow. "Yeah man, your sister put me on my ass."

I stood over him, still watching to make sure he was okay. "I'm sorry."

"For what?" He laughed as my brother helped him up to his feet.

"Careful…" I put my hands on each side of his waist to make sure he was steady. "For going so rough. I shouldn't have."

"London, I'm a hockey player, I can handle it," he said. "Plus, it was kinda hot to see you in competitive mode like that."

"Don't think I won't drop you on your ass, man. That's my sister, not some hockey ho," Trent joked.

"Right, right," Pratt agreed, and winked at me.

Mom had just made it to us, and my dad was right behind her, walking over to my snowbie.

"Pratt, sweetie," Mom said. "Are you okay? London, I can't believe you went all out on him like that. You should have known better. Do you need to go to the hospital?" Her words rushed out in a quick string.

"Nah, I think I'll be alright, Mrs. S. Nothing broken," Pratt replied. "Could have been a lot worse."

My dad asked if Pratt was okay, and my mom gave him a thumbs up. *Such dorks, but I love them.* My dad hopped on the snowbie and started it up, then took off towards the barn. The rest of us headed carefully for the house, taking it slow for Pratt.

As we approached the back door, Pratt asked me to stay behind for a sec, and Trent looked back at us.

"L, you cool?" he asked.

"She's fine, man. Like I'd ever put the mack on your sister," Pratt laughed.

"Oh, I'm sure you wouldn't," Trent smirked.

"Come on, inside. Leave them be." My mom guided him towards the door. "You know she could do a lot worse than Pratt," I heard her tell him in a really loud whisper.

I laughed and turned to Pratt. "What's up?"

"Thank you," he said.

"Um, you're welcome? And you couldn't tell me that inside why?" I joked.

"I guess I just like how pink your nose is outside." He touched it with his pointer finger and gave me some dimple. His smile was growing on me. Not like it was difficult. He had a great smile, and he was pretty hot.

That dimple will kill me. I'm a sucker for the dimple. And I think I just admitted that he's hot.

"Whatever. I'm just glad you're all right. Let me see that again." I stood on the step so I could be eye-level with him. "You can take the ice pack off now."

I lifted his hand and got in closer to take a better look. "It doesn't look broken, thank God. But we do need to take care of that cut. I'm assuming it's just a cut, because it didn't bleed too much."

I ran my thumb gently across it, and he took my hand then kissed it.

Oh hell, Mr. Montgomery…you do have a charming side.

"Alright, Eighty-Six. Maybe you hit your head harder than I thought." I tried my best to sound playful, to try and hide the shakiness of my voice. *Fail.*

"Nah, my head is right on target." He searched my eyes and I knew at that moment I had it bad. It turned out Eighty-Six was a perfect ten.

Chapter 5

Having Pratt around was a bunch of things all rolled into one. He was a huge pain in the ass, but also sweet and funny, then annoying as all hell…then he'd turn around and make up for all that mess with something genuine. I didn't ask about his family anymore after the night in the loft. I figured he'd talk about it when he was ready.

Christmas was in one week. I hadn't got a single gift yet because of the snow, but the roads were finally cleared, so I needed to get to the mall. Trent and Pratt were out with my dad playing a pick up game at the ice rink with his old rec team, and my mom's friend was picking her up to go to a fundraiser, so she left me the keys to her car. I had the rest of the day all to myself.

After I got out of the shower I started to get dressed, but realized my jeans were in the dryer. I quickly wrapped a towel around myself and ran downstairs to get them. The dryer was still running but I pulled them out anyhow, burning my palm on the button.

"Holy hell, how do these get so damn hot?" I questioned out loud as I walked out of the laundry room to head back upstairs.

As I rounded the corner, I saw a shadow. I froze. *Everyone's out. Who the hell is that? Stranger Danger. Stranger Danger.* I glanced around me to see if there was something I could pick up and swing at whoever it was. *Damn you Trent, for years you left hockey sticks everywhere…* I swiped the foot-tall wooden drummer boy nutcracker off the counter and lifted it over my head to swing. The next string of events happened in such an unstoppable and rapid succession, I wasn't even sure it was actually happening until it was too late. As I started to swing, I was happy to see it was Pratt and not an intruder, so I stopped mid-swing…but my towel had other plans. It dropped to the floor.

I know I wasn't standing there in my panties very long, but it was long enough that Pratt got a glimpse of 'the girls', as well as my ass when I screamed, turned away and bent over to grab the towel. As I bolted up the stairs, without my jeans *of course,* I heard him call after me. Before I heard the knock on my door I put my T-shirt on and looked for a pair of anything to cover up.

"London. London. It's no biggy. I've seen boobies before. Can I come in?" I could hear the amusement in his voice.

Shit.

"Suck it, Eighty-Six," I called out.

"Just give me the chance," he shot back, and by his tone I could tell he had that stupid adorable grin plastered across his damn face. That grin made my stomach twirl with excitement.

"I have your jeans out here."

"I have another pair. Thanks."

"Open the door, London. Please?"

I knew I shouldn't, but I did. I opened the door slowly and peeked out. When I saw him holding my jeans I opened it all the way. That's when I noticed he was standing there in his boxers and socks. I instantly busted out in laughter and reached to take my jeans from him. But instead of allowing me to take them, he opened his hand and grabbed mine. This was not helping the situation happening in my stomach, amongst other places. *Ah shit London…steady, girl. I know it's been a while, but focus.*

"Thank you. Now go put on your pants, Eighty-Six." I attempted to pull my hand back, but he gripped it just slightly tighter.

He grinned. "Go put *your* pants on, Princess."

"I'm trying." I tugged at them again.

He pulled his hand back a little harder, causing me to jerk forward against him. I didn't look up right away. I stared at his neck, which I was eye-level with. I could feel my heart racing – or maybe it was his. I couldn't tell, we were so close. I knew that if I made eye contact with him, it'd be over. He lowered his right hand and dropped my jeans, then slid his arm around me, stopping at the small of my back. I could feel the trail of his touch still lingering as he pulled me in closer. *Oh Lord, his chest…his arms…his abs…his boxers are looking a bit full too. Jesus, London, do something.* I ran my hand up his chest and rested it on his shoulder.

"Pratt…I," I began, and then stopped. I didn't *know* what to say. He was rubbing his hand back and forth against my back when he put his forehead against the top of my head.

"I didn't come up here expecting anything, London. In hindsight maybe the whole boxer thing was a bad idea. I thought if I were practically naked you'd feel better about me seeing you. Like we'd be even on the naked playing field type thing. I'm sorry. I'm an idiot. I didn't intend to give you the impression I expected something from you. I was just trying to make you feel better by doing something funny for you." He began to pull back, but I didn't let him. I looked up, and I could see a glimpse of embarrassment in his eyes.

"You are not an idiot," is all I could muster up before I pulled him down to me and kissed him. I pushed up against him until his back was to the wall, and wrapped my arms around his neck. I was on my tippy toes, so when I started to lose my balance he ran his hands down my back, allowing them to linger on my ass for a few seconds before sliding them down a little bit further and grabbing the backs of my thighs. He squeezed with just enough pressure to pick me up, sending my insides into a frenzy. When he moved away from the wall I wrapped my legs around him, and he walked us into my room.

I pushed the door shut behind him, and then ran my fingers through his hair until I had two handfuls of it. When we got to the bed I let go of him and climbed in. He groaned with pleasure and stood over me as I lay there awaiting his touch, in utter pleasure mixed with the pure ache of wanting him.

"I've wanted to kiss you since the day I laid eyes on you, London," he whispered, practically out of breath. "If this gets to be too much, just say the word. I don't need you thinking that this was my plan all along." He looked so serious – no dimple, not even a trace of a smile.

Does he think I don't want this? I do, but…all right, here goes.

"Let's just keep it NC-17 for tonight, okay?" I suggested. "That way there's no pressure or mixed signals."

He was quiet for a moment or two, then he smirked and shook his head.

"I've never met anyone like you."

"I could say the same about you," I countered.

"This is a new one. Setting up boundaries beforehand? You know exactly who you are, don't you?" His expression was wide-eyed and filled with excitement.

"I'm workin' on it."

"Amazing," he breathed, before he leaned down to kiss me. I broke away from him to sit up, and began trailing soft kisses over his abs, then ran my hands around his waist and down over his boxers. He tensed up and groaned again. His hands wound through my hair then to my face, tilting it up, and he leaned down and kissed me. I pulled away and slid to the top of my bed. I needed him to know I was just as into this as he seemed to be. I removed my shirt and called him over with the crook of my finger.

At first he just stood there, and I wondered if he was having second thoughts, but then his smile grew wide. He climbed on to the bed and lay down next to me. His lips found mine while he ran his hand down my stomach and stopped at the top of my panties. By that time I was about to bust with frustration, so I nudged him with my hips. That's all it took. His hand began to move again and he kissed me like I'd never been kissed before.

Pratt Montgomery has a sexy-as-hell side.

I had fallen asleep, and when I woke my nose was buried in Pratt's neck. He was on his side facing me, with one arm stretched out under me and the other resting on my side. I fit in there perfectly. I slid myself out and tried to move quietly to go use the bathroom, but he opened his eyes and grinned.

"Sneaking off on me, Princess?"

I leaned over and stole a quick kiss. "I gotta pee."

"Everyone's home now," he informed me. "Just so you know."

"What? Why didn't you leave, then?"

"Well, your jeans make my ass look big, so I couldn't go anywhere." He was clearly amused by his own joke, judging by his devilish grin.

I slapped his arm lightly and laughed quietly. "You got jokes, huh Eighty-Six?" I teased.

"Well, my clothes aren't in here, remember? Boxers only." He pointed to his lack of apparel.

"Right. Shit. Okay. When I go to the bathroom I'll grab them. Where are they?" I found my shirt, then took a pair of shorts out of my drawer and put them on.

"Trent's room, on the floor behind the door." He sat up and extended his arm, and I went to him. He fiddled with my fingers, not looking up. "What will you say if he asks where I am?"

"Nothing. I can ignore Trent, or lie." I answered. "Besides, it's none of his business." I shrugged and closed the door behind me.

After I used the bathroom I ran down the hall, grabbed the pile of clothing behind Trent's door, and headed back to my room. I opened the door and threw them at Pratt, told him I'd be downstairs, and asked him to give it a few minutes before coming down.

Nobody even asked where Pratt was, and when he finally did come down my dad assumed he'd been napping. Apparently, that was the excuse he'd used to get out of the pick up game – he was tired. It was so hard to keep a straight face while he talked to them. I was right back to four hours ago, before things officially changed between us.

To make sure I didn't give anything away with my facial expressions, I went back upstairs to get ready to go shopping. I found myself thinking about how things had changed so quickly. I tried to pinpoint when, but I couldn't. It was like this snowball rolling downhill, getting bigger and bigger with every passing second. Each new thing he surprised me with, I found myself liking him more and more.

I pulled some clean clothes out of my drawer and put them on, then went to brush my teeth. While brushing I stared back at myself in the mirror and laughed, thinking about what Lola had said right before I left: "*Go get laid or something.*" Well, I had the *or something* part covered. When Pratt and I were together earlier, all we'd done was mess around. I'm not a first date type of chick. I'm not even a second or third date kind of chick. I have to think you're going to stick around a while if I'm giving it up. I guess that's why I hadn't had very much of that over the last four years.

And that was also why I'd worried when I first started to get that anxious feeling in my belly when Eighty-Six came in a room or touched me. Up until today, he had only touched me when I was about to bust my ass or when I was handing him his ass on a snow tube. I'm sure being a good-looking guy and a star hockey player presented him with opportunities now and again. *Ha. Now and again? Try all the time.* I'd been worried that would be an issue, but it wasn't. He didn't even try – he'd let me set the boundaries. When it came to him, they were hard even for *me* to stick to, and they were my own rules. Talk about inner conflict.

I grabbed my purse and went back downstairs. "Dad, I'm going to the mall," I shouted in the direction of the living room. I heard him call out goodbye, and then I found the guys in the kitchen.

"Hold up," Trent said. "We're going to Hat Trick's later on – wanna go?"

Pratt was leaning on the counter eating an apple. "Yeah Princess, wanna go?" He winked at me and I hid my smile by pretending I was looking for something in my purse.

"Sounds good. I'll be back by nine," I answered, before I walked out the door.

As I started the car my text alert went off. It was Pratt, sending me one of the selfies we took together before I fell asleep. I had to admit, we were pretty cute together. My mom was right. I could do a lot worse than Pratt – because he was setting the standard pretty damn high.

Chapter 6

As I walked around the mall checking everything out, I was having a difficult time trying to find something for my mom. Everyone else around me made it look so easy. One lady walked by me, barely able to hold the bags she had, and the three kids with her had their hands full as well. I did enjoy watching people shop at the holidays. The way their faces light up when they find the perfect gift for someone, or how husbands cringe when they enter a store because they know what's about to go down. Or the ones who know there's no sense in fighting it, so they follow behind carrying packages and bags. I lived within my means all year long, which wasn't much, but I made for damn sure I always put money away for the holidays. I enjoyed gift giving.

My dad was easy peasy to shop for. I get him a new sweater every year – it's all he wants. I changed it up one year, and he looked disappointed. Of course he said he wasn't, but I could tell. Now 2009 is referred to as the 'London got Dad a wallet' year. But Mom was much harder. I think it was because she loved so many things. What I really wanted to get her was a day at a spa or something, but she isn't into that stuff. So instead I was stuck with what I knew – which ended up being a turquoise necklace with matching earrings and a bracelet. Also, two knitted fluffy neck wraps. She really needed to be bundled up when it was cold. I knew she'd love them. Trent was like shopping for a ten-year-old child – video games and a hockey jersey was all he required to appease him on Christmas morning. It may have sounded mundane, but they always loved their gifts.

Then my 'family' gift was a picture of us all, from when we were visiting with Jon, a college hockey buddy of my dad's, and his wife Terri. We stayed with them at their 'off the grid' cabin up by the Boundary Waters. It was right after my mom had been cleared the second time, and we went up there to unwind for two weeks. I was having it made into a big mounted canvas print for our den. When I went in to drop off the picture I had to fill out some paperwork and wait for the guy to get back with my written receipt for payment and pick up. While I waited, I was messing with my phone, and decided to set the pic that Pratt sent me as my wallpaper. I'd never done anything like that before so it felt really strange, but satisfying at the same time. I thought maybe I was acting too fast or desperate…but I ultimately decided I was just behaving like a happy person did. It wasn't as if people were ever in my phone, anyhow.

While I was fiddling around with my settings I got a text alert. It was Trent, asking when I'd be back. They were hungry, and wanted to get out of the house already. I texted him back that I was leaving in ten minutes. I'd finished shopping for everyone, so it didn't bug me that he was rushing me. I'd even managed to get Pratt something on such short notice. I had planned to get him a membership to the Jelly of the Month Club before I got to know him. Lucky for him he graduated to flannel – I got him a new flannel shirt. In all honesty, I was being selfish. Technically, that was a gift for *me*, being how much I enjoyed watching him wear one.

As I pulled into the driveway I saw him sitting on the front porch steps, looking down at the ground. It wasn't until I got out and began walking towards him that I realized he was on the phone.

"I gotta go. I'll talk to you later." He stood and slid his phone into his pocket. "Hey there. Here, let me help you." He took the bags out of my hands and looked behind him.

"What's wrong?" I moved my head to look behind him, but he gave me a quick kiss before I could see anything.

"Nothing's wrong. I just wanted to make sure nobody was looking," he said with a smile. Just then Tuna came barging out the storm door and right to me. Luckily he didn't knock me over this time. I gave him a pat on the head, then headed inside with Pratt right behind me.

"Hey kids," my mom greeted us from the kitchen.

We went in to see her. "Hey, Mom. How was the fundraiser luncheon?" I replied.

"Hey, Mrs. S," Pratt said.

"Pratt, how many times do I need to tell you? Please, sweetheart, call me Linda." She sounded exasperated.

"Mom, you okay?" I rushed over to her.

"Oh yeah, I'm fine. I was just looking for Nana's banana pudding recipe, and, well…I realized the cabinets were an unorganized nightmare. The luncheon was great. Had a nice time seeing everyone." She waved her hand as if to dismiss it. Even though she was cancer-free, she still had immune issues from all the past treatments, and she tired easily. It was a small price to pay to have her here, but she got frustrated sometimes.

"Where's Trent?" Pratt asked.

"Trent's here," my brother answered as he came down the stairs.

Pratt took off his hat and rubbed the back of his head, sending his shaggy curls into disarray. He looked stressed out. "Man, I don't want to go out tonight. How about tomorrow? I just want to stay in and chill. Watch a movie or something."

"You've gotta' be shitting me, dude. We've been in this house for six days now. We *need* to get out for a while."

"You were just out with Dad, you fool," I pointed out to him. "Don't even try the cabin fever shenanigans."

"Exactly. Out with *Dad*," Trent said through his teeth, and widened his eyes.

"Well, I'm tired," I said. "Shopping and the crowds wore me out. Tomorrow would work better for me, too. Plus, Friday nights are two-dollar drafts. That's more your style, eh?" I played it cool, trying to convince him.

"Fine," Trent agreed. "But don't bail on me again." He grabbed a banana and headed back upstairs. I could see the tension ease from Eighty-Six's face, and his knuckles start to unclench.

"Trent, give me back that banana," Mom shouted after him. "It's for Nana's recipe."

"You can't even find it, Mom," he teased her as he ran up the stairs.

"He has a point," she conceded.

When my parents went off to bed I decided to catch up on one of my shows, binge style. I could hear the guys in Trent's room, yelling things like 'get my flank and RPG you dumbass'. Either they were playing a video game, or they were saving the world right from the bedroom. *I'm way more fun than saving the world. Stupid boys and their stupid toys.* I hoped Pratt would make it down to hang out with me at some point after he was done playing.

I showered, made a salad, and grabbed some water before heading to the den to start my binge-a-thon. About an hour into it I went to use the bathroom, and when I came back Eighty-Six was on the couch reading the info about my show.

"Hey you," I greeted him. I was surprised to see him – I'd started to think he'd be up there with Trent all night.

"The president is having an affair with the speechwriter and there's a spy in the White House threatening to expose them all unless his uncle is freed from a maximum security prison on Mars run by aliens who suck the life out of humans to fuel their own worldly needs?" He laughed. "What kind of crazy shit is this?"

"There are no aliens, doofus," I joked.

"Come here." He wrapped his arms around my waist and pulled me down on his lap. I felt so tiny with his arms around me, like he could ball me up and shove me in his pocket. I felt…happy.

"I'm glad you could take a break from the war you were waging upstairs with Trent," I teased him.

He smirked. "I was thinking of you the entire time."

"While you were blowing people up or yelling at the 14-year-olds on the other end of the mic to suck it up buttercup, your mommy ain't here to protect you. Go in and shoot that mofo' like a soldier." I laughed while I repeated something along the lines of what I heard him say earlier.

"Ah, touché Princess. You've seen the monster in me," he joked, and squeezed me tighter. "Thanks for helping me out earlier." He gave me a kiss.

"Yeah, no problem. I could tell something was bothering you. Wanna talk about it?" I asked cautiously. I didn't know if he was a talker or a stuffer, and I didn't want to push him too hard.

"It's nothing really. My aunt called to let me know someone stopped by her house to see me, and was asking how I was. It caught her off-guard was all, and she wanted to let me know." He shrugged his shoulders.

He has an aunt who's still alive. That's good news. I wonder why he isn't with her.

"Is she upset that you're here?" I asked.

"No. We haven't seen each other in a while. I stayed with her for about a week after the accident, and then I went back to school. I know she loves me…" He paused and exhaled loudly. "It's just hard for her to look at me because I resemble my father *so* much…her brother. I'm sort of a constant reminder that our entire family was wiped out in the blink of an eye."

"I'm sorry, I didn't mean to pry. I'll shut up now." I tried to climb off his lap but he held on to me.

"You aren't prying, London. You're caring. I like caring." He gave a small, thin-lipped smile. "It's been a while since someone cared." He buried his face in my neck and squeezed me tight.

Oh shit. Is he okay? London, keep him talking because if he cries or explodes you won't know what to do.

"Don't cry on me, please," I blurted – and was immediately mortified to hear that coming out of my mouth. *Smooooooth London, fucking smooooth.* "I mean…I…I didn't mean it like.... aahhh fuck. I don't know what I meant. I'm sorry. I panicked." I stuttered through the sentence like a bumbling idiot.

"I have *no* idea what you're going on about, but don't worry. I'm not going to cry." He looked at me and gave a laugh.

"My family adores you, Pratt. You'll always be welcome here….no matter what." I added the 'no matter what' because if things didn't go anywhere with us, or if this was just some vacation fling thing to him, I didn't want him to feel like he couldn't come back.

"You hesitated," he said, and his breath tickled my neck. I squirmed and laughed.

"I hesitated?"

"Yeah, as if you were unsure about me and you. You know…'no matter what'." He quoted my words back at me.

"I didn't want to jump to conclusions and cause more stress for you…pressure you into something. I don't know. I was just being cautious." I shrugged, and he lifted his head and pressed his forehead against mine.

"Who'd have ever thought, Princess?" His eyes crinkled up like he was smiling.

"I know, right?" I agreed and stood up; his arms were still locked behind my back though, so I couldn't go far. As he pulled me in again I straddled him, then wrapped my arms around his neck.

"This is going to be too easy," he said.

"Hey now! Too easy?" I smacked his arm. I wasn't sure if I should be angry, offended or laughing.

"Oh. No, not like that. I'm sorry. My think-to-speak button is busted. Not like *that,* London. What I meant was, too easy to fall in love with you." He said it soft and close to my lips…and then he kissed me. He kissed me like his being depended on it, and it made me feel as if I was the most important person in the world to him. Like I mattered in so many more ways than just a fling. He kissed me like we had a future together.

Oh Lord, save me. Pratt Montgomery, you're making it too easy on me *now.*

Chapter 7

I woke to the sensation of the couch shaking and the sound of my brother's voice. By the time I was alert enough to open my eyes, I didn't want to. The couch kept shaking though, like something was being bounced off of it.

"Quit kicking me, man," Pratt said loudly. "What's your problem?"

"My problem is you're sprawled out on the couch with my sister sprawled out on *you.*" Trent's voice was louder.

"Trent, stop," I said. "It's not what you think. We were binge watching 'A Presidential Affair' and we fell asleep. I must have just gotten comfortable while I was sleeping."

Trent looked at Pratt while Pratt looked at me. I didn't make any moves or facial expressions – I just sat waiting for him to answer my brother.

"Yeah man, I'm sorry. It wasn't like that at all," Pratt said. "We just conked out." He sounded convincing enough.

"Ahh, I'm just busting chops. I don't care, dude. London's a big girl and uses good judgment. Besides, you're a good guy." Trent gave Pratt a slap on the shoulder.

That's surprising; I guess Trent knew I could do a lot worse than Pratt too.

"Just don't hurt him, London," Trent added.

"Wait, what?" I laughed. "You're a dickhead."

"You guys should get out of here, though, unless you want Mom to come down here and see this. Not that she'd be upset – the exact opposite actually, but I don't know if Pratt's ready for *that* level of Mom yet." He smirked as he left the room.

"What time is it?" I asked Pratt.

He pulled his phone out of his pocket to check. I wasn't looking, but I couldn't help but notice the '18 New Texts' alert across the screen.

"One-thirty." He stuck his phone back in his pocket and slid out from under me to sit upright. I sat up too, wondering if he was moving away from me for a reason. Maybe Trent scared him off with the whole Mom comment, or perhaps it had something to do with the eighteen texts he'd missed. *Cool it. You aren't a jealous person. At least you never were.*

"I need a drink and the bathroom." He lightly slapped my knee and stood, offering his hand to help me up. I took it and stood up too, then picked up my mess from earlier.

"Goodnight," he said to me, and kissed my forehead before leaving the room.

Boo. No more Eighty-Six for the night.

I went to the kitchen to wash the dishes I'd used. After I finished, Tuna came in looking for a treat.

"You are such an oinker, Tuna. Did you come all the way down here just because you knew I'd give you a treat?" I laughed and petted him.

Just as I was turning off the light to head to bed, Tuna's ears popped up slightly. I stopped to listen, and could hear a faint muffled voice coming from upstairs. It didn't get any clearer as I went up the steps – it was just a slightly louder muffled voice behind running water. Whoever it was didn't want anyone to know what was being said, that's for sure. Maybe it was Pratt – he'd said he needed the bathroom. That's when the water shut off and I could hear the voice more clearly. I contemplated running down the hall to my brother's room to see who was missing, then I told myself I was being ridiculous. Whoever it was, it was none of my business. If they wanted anybody to know, they wouldn't have gone through all that to hide it…at nearly two a.m.

"I'll see you when I come to visit." There was a pause. "Yes, soon. I've *got* to go, Trent needs the bathroom."

Well, that settled it. That was for sure Pratt doing the talking. Somewhere in the three seconds I got lost in my thoughts, the door swung open, and then my brother was standing in front of me with Pratt right behind him.

"Jesus Christ, London. How long have you been standing there? You scared the fuck out of me," Trent whisper yelled as Pratt handed his phone back.

I was really confused but I didn't want to ask any questions. I was embarrassed enough getting caught eavesdropping…even though I didn't hear squat.

What the hell were they doing in there together, making some super-secret phone call?

"I needed the bathroom." That was the simplest answer I could come up with without coming off as a snooping snooper that snoops. Even though I was snooping…kind of sort of, in an inadvertent way.

I went back to my room after I pretended to use the bathroom and threw my pants in the hamper so I was comfy for sleep.

Sleep. Yeah, right.

I wondered who Pratt was talking with that he would tell them he'd see them soon? And why was he using Trent's phone? His seemed to work fine earlier. I didn't know enough about his past to make any assumptions, so I tried my best to forget about the eighteen texts and the mystery phone call and go to sleep.

But that didn't work so well. I found myself thinking about Pratt and how he was just down the hall from me. This was so easy it was hard for me to grasp. Never, ever had I connected with someone the way I was connecting with Pratt. Most everyone I'd dated I knew from grade school and up. I never really dated 'out of the box' except for a few guys my sophomore year. Always seemed after the fifth date, if I would give in to my own wants as well, I never really heard from them again. *Alright, not completely true.* That may have happened with one guy and I sort of expected it. I was totally okay with it. The others though, I may have blocked their phone number once or twice when they'd get too needy. I had a plan to follow, and I didn't want or need to drag any extra baggage around with me.

My phone went off, making me jump a little. It was him.

Can I come in? ☺

Sure.

As soon as I hit send on my reply, my heart began to race and my stomach was in a state of that blissful turmoil. *He wants to see me.*

My door opened, and I could see his shadow in the moonlight from my window. Tuna gave a grumpy grumble at the interruption, and went out. Then Pratt shut the door behind him.

He stood next to my bed, shirtless, and I sat up. His lickable abs were right at my eye level as he ran his hands through his hair and left them folded on top of his head, exhaling with what seemed like frustration. Even in the dim light I could see he wasn't okay.

"L, I…" he began.

I didn't want him to say anything else. It was nearly two-thirty in the morning and it seemed like a lot had happened in the hour since we woke up on the couch. I didn't want to think about anything, and I wanted to take whatever was bothering him off his mind…at least for a little while.

I pushed the covers back, then slipped a hand into the waistband of his shorts and pulled him towards me. "Want to keep me warm?"

"You aren't mad?" He cocked his head to the side with a surprised expression.

"Mad? At what?" I asked. I mean I was curious, yes, but mad? No.

"The bathroom phone call," he said flatly.

"A, not my business. B, it wasn't my intention to eavesdrop. And C, I didn't hear anything. So no, I'm not mad." I gave a quick laugh, trying to convince him that I was okay, because I really didn't want to talk about it.

"London, let me explain," he said as he got into bed. He lay on his side facing me and slid his arm under my pillow.

"I. Don't. Care." I kissed his lips after each word. Then I ran my hand around his side, up his back to his shoulder, then down his arm.

He tried again. "But…"

"Shhh, please?" I cut him off. "I'm exhausted." Then I lifted my head up to kiss him again. That time I made sure the last thing he'd want to do was talk.

It was as if I'd relieved him of something that was bugging him. Either that, or he was holding waaaay back on me earlier. His hand found my hair and his lips took over mine. His breathing was getting faster and heavier. *Holy shit, what a turn-on.*

I was loving every second of it…but the bad thing was, I knew with this level of attraction, physically and mentally, there was a snowball's chance in hell of me keeping to my own rules. The good thing about that was, I didn't care. Maybe those weren't so much *rules,* but instincts instead. I felt like I knew Pratt wasn't going anywhere. Even after break was over. There was something more there than just a Christmas crush or a holiday hook-up. That's how I felt about him, anyhow, but the beauty of it all was I didn't need any of those excuses. I wanted him, *bad,* and that was enough of a reason for me to throw all my fears out the window.

Before I knew it, my shirt was over my head and his shorts were off. My hands wandered everywhere on his body as his mouth moved to my neck and his hand slid up my stomach to my breast. I could feel him against me through his boxers, which turned me on even more. I ran my hand over his chest, down over his abs, and found him. He moaned my name into my neck, which sent me over the edge. I guided his hand down to my panties, and he tugged at them, so I lifted up. Once he got them down far enough I wiggled out of them using my feet. When I stilled, his fingers explored me. I was ready. I wanted him. *All of him.* I was desperate for his touch. I wanted him all over me.

But he stopped touching me, and gently pulled my hand away from him.

"Hold on, hold on." He was out of breath.

Hold on? What? No. No. No.

"Hey. Open your eyes," he said with a small laugh, and moved the hair away from my face.

I wasn't ready for the eye-opening part, but I did as he asked anyhow. He was propped up on his elbow, looking concerned.

"What are we doing?" he asked. "Are we good?"

"If I have to tell you what we're doing and how we're doing, I *really* overestimated you." I stuck my tongue out at him and laughed. He threw his head back and laughed quietly along with me.

"Boundaries, limits. Give 'em to me. I need to come up with my plan of attack."
He emphasized the word *attack* and went for my neck, and I tried my best to pull him on
top of me. Luckily he got the hint to move in between my legs. But then he held himself
up with his arms over me, hesitating.

"How about this?" I said. "Don't talk, just do. If I don't stop you…don't stop.
Don't ask if I'm sure…don't think about anything. Just. Do."

He nodded with a crooked grin and then kissed me. I wrapped my legs around
him, but pulled away from his kiss.

"Wait – do me a quick favor?" I asked.

"Sure." He pulled back and sat up on his knees.

I pointed to the small end table next to my bed. "Go in that drawer right there and
get me the little blue bag. Just give me what's in it, please."

He reached over and pulled out the bag. When he opened it I could see his dimple
was back, with that adorable grin of his. He handed me the condoms.

"Don't think. Just do." I reminded him, and pulled him back down to me.

Chapter 8

I woke to a very naked Pratt draped over me, and I didn't care that it was 110 degrees under him. I was happy as could be and wanted to stay that way all day with him. After I'd used the bathroom earlier, I locked the door so nobody could just walk in. I ran my fingers up his back and over his shoulder and then down the back of his arm that was across my chest. I repeated this a couple of times mindlessly until I noticed he stirred a bit and twitched when I went over certain spots. When I laughed he jumped up, scaring the shit out of me. Just as fast, he was on top of me, pinning me down by my wrists.

"Oh, so you want to play tickle tickle, huh Princess?" he joked.

I started laughing and wiggled under him, trying to break loose, but he had his full weight down on me. The air came whooshing out of my lungs as he let go of my wrists and kissed me. When he slipped his arm behind my head and hitched up my left leg, bringing us closer, I could feel him against me. Instantly my body reacted and I couldn't believe how I needed him. We must have looked like we were wrapped in a mess of Christmas lights or something, the way we were tangled up in each other. He pulled away from me, then started at my neck and worked his way down… *Oh my.* Within seconds I had the pillow over my face to muffle the sounds of my pleasure. I could feel him moving around while he was down there. I was lost on the verge of an orgasm…then suddenly he was in me. I didn't expect it, so I screamed. He took the pillow off of my face and got close to my ear.

"You okay?" He stilled, breathing heavily.

I couldn't exactly form words at that moment, so I nodded as I nudged against him. That's all he needed to know – if I was good, he was good. And oh yeah, I was good all right.

Breakfast was awkward, to say the least. My dad had already eaten and taken off to go bring my aunt some things and check on her. Pratt and I sat at opposite ends of the kitchen table eating our food, while my mom eyed us up. Back and forth, back and forth, she'd sip her coffee then start all over again. With a shit-eating-grin. I didn't exactly like my eggs with a side of 'my mother knows I had sex'.

I need to text Lola and let her know I completed the bucket list she made for me. Dreamboat – check. Knock the dust out – check. Dreamboat knocks the dust out in parent's home – check, check, and check. The trifecta. Lola would be proud.

Pratt got up to put his plate in the sink, then his phone rang. He excused himself, and answered it in the living room. The floor plan of the house was open downstairs so it wasn't like he got much privacy. From the sound of his conversation, it was his aunt again.

"I know. I miss them too," he said quietly, and sat on the arm of the couch. "It's only been a little over a year. It's still fresh for you…for all of us." His voice cracked a bit.

At that point I just felt like I was intruding on a private family moment. I looked at my mom and signaled for us to leave the room. She agreed, but when we reached the steps Pratt whispered my name loudly. I turned and he waved me over to him. I looked at my mom, and she waved me off.

"Go be with him. He needs you." She gave a sympathetic smile and headed down the hall.

When I reached Pratt he put his arm around my waist and brought me in close to him, kissing my forehead. I turned my head to look for Mom but she was already gone.

"Aunt Simone. Calm down. Listen to me," he said, and then took a long pause. "I understand how you're feeling. If you want to blame yourself then I'd have to blame myself too. It was *my* game they were going to. But I know it wasn't my fault. It's the fault of the asshole who was too busy texting while driving his semi."

He took my hand and moved to the couch. He put his arm around me, and I leaned into him with my knees up and feet under me to the side. He was on the phone for about five more minutes, mostly quiet for the rest of the conversation. When he finished he put the phone in his pocket and exhaled.

"You okay?" I asked.

"Not really. I love my aunt but when she gets on the 'it's my fault' tangent it's usually because she's drunk or it's a holiday…or both," he muttered.

"Why does she blame herself? If you don't mind telling me, that is. If not that's cool. I completely understand," I said.

"Because they were on their way to pick her up before the game. Had they gotten off the exit for the university they'd never have been where they got hit. Right before her exit."

He looked at me with the saddest eyes, and it broke my heart that I couldn't help him.

"I miss my family, London. I miss them so much." He broke down and hugged me…hard.

Before, I thought if he lost it on me I wouldn't be able to deal with it, but I was so wrong. I simply hugged him back and ran my fingers through his hair to try and soothe him. My brother walked through the front door, but Pratt made no attempt to move. Trent looked at me with a concerned expression and I mouthed 'family' to him. He didn't understand what I was saying, so I just waved him off. Pratt sat up and wiped his face with his sleeve, then got up.

"I need the bathroom," he said, and walked out down the hall.

Trent slunk over to me. "What happened?"

"His aunt called. She was upset, which made him upset."

"Damn, it's got to be so rough on him," Trent sympathized.

"I bet," I said. "I know what it feels like to *almost* lose a parent but damn, your entire family? Pure hell."

"Well, we'll go out and have some fun tonight." Trent clapped and rubbed his hands together like it was his evil plan of action.

"Hat Trick's it is," I agreed.

I didn't want to hover and be a pain in the ass, but I did want to make sure Eighty-Six was okay, so I went along to the downstairs bathroom. When I saw it wasn't occupied, I checked the one upstairs. The door was closed, so I knocked.

"Pratt. You okay?" I said through the door. I waited a few moments, and when he didn't answer I knocked again. "Pratt?"

"I'm good, L. Be out in a few," he sniffed. Then I heard the shower start.

Before I walked away the door cracked open.

"You know, I'd invite you in but I don't think that's cool in your parents' house." He gave a weak smile. I stuck my face to the crack and gave him a kiss.

"You wouldn't have had the chance to invite me if they weren't home." I smiled sweetly then walked backwards away from him.

"You're killin' me, Princess." He gave me a quirked-up corner of the lips and squinted at me devilishly.

"I aim to please." I puckered up my lips and made a kissing noise. I was happy that at least he was smiling.

The rest of the day was spent out shopping some more with the family. The guys went in my dad's truck with him, while my mom and I took her car. I knew what was coming, so I just sat back and waited for it. But when she didn't say much the first few minutes, it started to bug me that she didn't ask. She was my mom. She was supposed to be nosy. I'm supposed to tell her these things.

"Mom?"

"Yeah, sweetie?" she answered.

"Anything on your mind?" I asked.

"Nothing in particular. Why do you ask?"

Okay, she had to be messing with me. I know she saw Pratt call me over to him, so why wasn't she asking questions?

"Just wondering. You're pretty quiet today."

"Just trying to give you the opportunity to tell me what's going on between you and Eighty-Six." She smirked and side-eyed me playfully.

"I like him. A lot, Mom," I blurted out. I never really held anything back with my mom. She was the easiest person to talk to and to get advice from. She never judged me – or at least if she did, she never made it known. She always kept a fair and respectful attitude towards anything we'd discuss, like when I wanted to change my major from architecture to biochem. The first thing she'd said then was, 'Hey, at least you didn't pick philosophy'. My mom was truly amazing.

"So is this just holiday hoopla happening, or do you two plan to try and take it outside of the house?" She chuckled. I didn't know if she was referring to Pratt and I trying to continue a relationship after winter break, or us having sex in the house. *Lola will be happy to know that's now officially on my favorite top ten things to do in my parents' home.*

I went with the first option.

"I don't know, too soon to tell I guess." I shrugged.

"He looks smitten with you, London," she said.

"Smitten, Mom?" I busted out laughing.

"He does. You should see how he looks at you. He watches you move. I've caught him giving a little smile when he thinks no one is looking. He needs someone – and I think maybe you could be it." I could hear the smile in her voice when she spoke.

"We'll see," I said, then straightened up in my seat because my phone was vibrating in my pocket. "Speak of the devil." I felt like a giddy teenager, fumbling with my phone to read his text.

Are you getting the Spanish Inquisition?

No. OMG is my dad drilling you?

No, Trent is. LOL

He's an idiot, just ignore him.

Yeah, I am. See ya in a few.

I put my phone in my pocket and sighed.

"Did you just sigh?" My mom laughed at me.

I sank in my seat, red-faced. "No. Yes. I don't know."

"London's got a crush," she sang like a schoolyard child.

Yep...London's got a crush.

We ended up staying at the mall for about two hours. We had some lunch, and then we all split up again to get the last of our shopping finished. I for sure wanted to get Pratt a few more things for under the tree. I couldn't imagine the heartache he'd be experiencing this Christmas, so the least I could do was show him that he had a second family, if he wanted it. That he'd never have to spend another holiday alone. Not as long as he didn't want to. I also stopped by the photo place to see if the picture was finished. Since it wasn't, I opted for them to deliver it to us for the extra fifteen bucks, and save myself a trip to that crowded hell again.

We all met back up, and as we were leaving the mall Trent got a text. He stopped short, then elbowed Eighty-Six in the arm. When Pratt stopped, Trent leaned over and then looked at me.

"What?" I mouthed to him as my parents were talking to each other. He shook his head as if to say 'nothing, don't worry about' it, so I minded my business. But then I saw Pratt look one way then the other, then tap Trent's shoulder and discreetly point towards the food court.

"Dad, can you ride home with Mom and Princess?" Trent asked, putting his phone back in his pocket. "We need to pick up something else that we forgot about."

I was curious as hell but didn't want to come off as psycho, so I kept my trap shut. Just as I was about to walk off, Pratt came over to me and leaned in to give me a quick kiss.

"I'll see you in a little bit," he said. "You and me have a date tonight."

"I guess we do, don't we?" I smiled, and he leaned in for another smooch right before he took off.

On the way out, my parents both teased me relentlessly about Eighty-Six laying a few kisses on me in public. Neither of them seemed surprised though – it was almost as if they wanted this to happen. *Hmmmmm.*

As soon as we got home I jumped in the shower. I wanted to clean up and take a nap before we went to Hat Trick's that night. It would be our first 'date', so I didn't want to be dirty and tired. By the time I was finished drying my hair I was exhausted, and fell asleep practically the instant my head hit the pillow.

I was woken up around six p.m. by Pratt slipping into bed with me. He wrapped his arms around me and kissed my head.

Oh, Mr. Montgomery. I could get used to this.

Chapter 9

I made sure I was ready before the guys, because I wanted to grab a snack before we left. I didn't plan on drinking much but I always did better with food in my stomach.

I was sort of nervous too. Why, I don't know. I mean, we had already moved past some of the most nerve-wracking firsts. First kiss...check. First bloody nose...check. First make out sesh...check. And of course the big S. Check. I had nothing to be nervous about, so I ate my oatmeal and almonds in an excited state while I waited for the guys to come down.

"Oatmeal, Princess?" Pratt kissed the top of my head, then opened the fridge and took out a bottle of water.

I stood and put my bowl in the sink and excused myself to brush my teeth really quick. On my way back from the bathroom I could hear Trent and Pratt talking in a hushed whisper.

"Dude, if she's in town we're in big shit," Trent said.

"I'm not worrying about it, man. If we ignore her, them, whoever, then they'll get tired of it and leave," Pratt reassured my brother.

Now I was really curious, and wondered if it had anything to do with what had happened earlier at the mall.

"All set?" I said as I rounded the corner.

"Yep. Let's go," Trent said, and took the keys to my dad's truck off the key rack.

"Can we take Mom's car, please?" I asked. "That way if you drink too much I can drive. You know I have a hard time with Dad's steering wheel – it's too hard for me to turn."

But Trent kept on walking with Dad's keys. "Eighty-Six can handle it. He isn't drinking tonight."

"Oh?" I questioned.

Pratt took out his phone and began typing as we got to the truck. My phone went off a second later.

"Really? A text?" I gave a quick laugh and spoke softly so my brother didn't hear. I pulled out my phone and checked the message.

I want to be sober for the after party.

We hopped in my dad's truck, all three of us in the front seat, me in the middle. *Yay.*

There's an after party? Where? I texted back.

In the barn loft.

Well, it was heated and insulated, so we wouldn't get cold. I worried about someone just walking in though, because you could see everything up there. But then again, who'd be walking in at two a.m.?

I love after parties.

And then my stomach began doing triple flips. I couldn't wait.

We walked into Hat Trick's and immediately I recognized people. Some I grew up with, some that I had classes with now, and a few new faces as well. Pratt took my hand and followed my brother through the crowd. He put me in between Trent and him without letting go. When we finally reached the bar area we got lucky – there was a small table open. I hopped up on the only available stool and put my clutch on the table, while Pratt and my brother stood.

"What do you want?" Trent yelled over the music and crowd noise.

"Grab a bucket of Coronas?" I asked him.

"Sure. I'll be back," he said, and took off to the bar. Pratt stood right next to me and rested his arm on the back of my stool.

"You look beautiful," he said in my ear. I could feel my cheeks getting hot, and I was feeling giddy.

"Thank you. You clean up pretty nice too, Eighty-Six," I whispered back.

He laughed, then leaned in to kiss me. *Kiss*, kiss me…and that was something new to me because I had never been big in the PDA department, but with Pratt, I found myself not giving two fucks. His hand fit perfectly around the back of my neck so when he'd slide it on back there and grip with just the right amount of pressure, it made me crazy. His demeanor would change when he'd take the back of my neck. It was like he pleasantly possessed me. Letting everyone know I was his. And *that* surprised the shit out of me as well. I never was one for being someone's bitch or marked like some slab of meat…but Pratt didn't make me feel like that. He made me feel wanted, and not in that 'let me in your pants' sort of way either.

When we finally separated, I saw my brother talking to a blonde-headed girl at the bar, and laughed.

"Looks like Trent is starting early. Least he could do was bring us our drinks back before he starts hitting on chicks." I nodded towards the bar.

Pratt turned to look, and his entire mannerism changed. He became rigid and pale. He ran his hands down his face, exhaling loudly, then slapped his hands on his thighs.

"You're kidding me," he said. "This is a fucking joke, right?"

"Are you asking me? Because I have no idea what you're taking about. Pratt, what's wrong?" I gently pulled his face in my direction.

"It's nothing," he told me. "I'll send your brother back over so you aren't alone." Then he walked off.

"Ooookay then…" *What just happened?*

I watched as my brother motioned to Pratt, pointing behind him, which I could only assume meant to walk away and come back over to me…but he didn't. He looked like he was arguing with Trent about something, and then Trent threw his hands up in the air with a pissed-off expression and walked towards me.

"Sooooo, what's happening right now?" I asked Trent when he reached the table.

"London. This was a big mistake," he said. "I should have known better. Let's get out of here." He grabbed my clutch and phone from the table.

"Wait. What do you mean? And what about Pra…."

But I didn't get to finish my question, because when I looked in Pratt's direction the blonde girl had taken his hand and was leading him through the crowd in the opposite direction. He didn't even look back to see if I was watching.

My stomach dropped – I couldn't believe what I was seeing. There *had* to be an explanation.

"Trent?" I looked at my brother, trying to hold back the tears that were building up.

"Let me get you out of here first." He took my hand and pulled me through the crowd to the exit. When we got outside I took a deep breath of the cold air, hoping I'd feel less suffocated and sick. But I was still in shock.

"What the fuck just happened? Seriously. Did I just see that? Who the hell was that, Trent?"

Just as my brother opened his mouth to answer me, the door opened and Hannah walked out. She gave me a nasty look, but then changed her attitude when she spoke to Trent directly.

"Oh good, you're still here. You going to bring her home and come back and hang out for a bit?"

"Fuck you, Hannah. All you and that bitch friend of yours do is ruin lives. Understand that, you dumb skank?" My brother had his fists balled at his sides and was practically yelling through clenched teeth, almost right in her face.

"Too bad, we could have taken a ride down memory lane." She winked at him and turned to go inside. Then she stopped and turned back to us.

"And don't worry about Pratt. Alexi will make sure he gets somewhere safe for the night." She gave a sarcastic grin that I wanted to smack off her face.

"What the fuck did you *do*, Hannah?" I yelled at her.

"Oh, nothing, *Princess*," she said. "Alexi just came to get back what was hers." Then she walked back inside.

"Trent, what does she mean?" I was starting to shake – mainly because I was cold, but I'd be lying if I didn't say it was also because I wanted to rip her face off and stuff it up her ass.

"Alexi is Pratt's ex-girlfriend. She left him, no shit, like maybe two weeks after his family was killed. She said she couldn't handle the stress of his 'emotional' mood swings." Trent took my arm and led me in the direction of the truck.

"Wait." I yanked my arm out of his grip. "There's no way we're leaving here without him, Trent." I started back to the entrance, and my brother started cussing like the father in 'A Christmas Story' when the Bumpus's dogs ate his Christmas turkey.

"London, don't. You don't understand… Shit. London."

But I kept walking. By the time he caught up with me I was already inside, headed in the direction Pratt had gone. Trent was right behind me, begging me to just leave it alone. Pratt would make it back to the house on his own. As I turned to tell him to shut up I caught a glimpse of a red hat. When I finally focused and saw that it was Pratt I wanted to vomit, and I hadn't even had a drink.

He had his back against the wall, and was kissing the blonde.

Trent pushed me aside and went to go after him. At first I was too shocked and sick to move, but I snapped out of it and just barely grabbed his arm.

"I'm going to kick his ass, London," Trent yelled.

"No. Stop. He can do whatever the fuck he wants," I said, fighting back the sting in my nose so I wouldn't cry. "He wasn't my boyfriend or anything. He's a single guy. Like you said, I'm sure he'll get back on his own. Let's go." *Stupid, stupid London.*

Before I turned to leave I stood there for another second, watching him. When he saw me he immediately took Alexi by the arms and pushed her away from him, and called after me.

"Go. Go, Trent!" I smacked his arm really fast as we pushed our way through the crowd again to leave.

"London...Trent..." Pratt called louder and louder. I ignored him and kept on going. I couldn't hold back the tears anymore – I had to wipe my eyes so I could see when we got to the truck.

"London, wait! I can..." Pratt began, but I got in the truck and slammed the door. My brother, on the other hand, opted otherwise.

"Stay the *fuck* away from her, Eighty-Six. I cannot believe you would do that to *her*. Of all people, *London*. My sister." Trent was yelling in Pratt's face. "We invited you into our home to share the holidays with us and *this* is how you show your appreciation? Just go, dude. Your shit will be on the front porch if you decide to come get it. Asshole. You're lucky she's so upset that I don't want to upset her more by kicking your ass." He pushed Pratt back away from the truck, and got in. "Just go, before I change my mind."

Pratt came to my window as Trent started the truck. It needed a second to warm up, so I was stuck when Pratt came to my window and begged me to listen to him. With his phone in his hand against the window I saw the picture of him and me on it as his wallpaper. That only upset me more and I squeezed my eyes shut for a moment, hoping I was just having a bad dream.

"London, it wasn't what you think. Please, just hear me out," he begged, with his forehead against the window.

I just sat staring straight ahead, not acknowledging him at all, but I could see he was looking up at me as I wiped my tears from my cheeks.

"Please, baby, listen to me," he begged again. "I swear it's not what you think."

"Fuck you," were the only two words that came out of my mouth before Trent pulled off, kicking up gravel and dirt in his wake.

I watched in the sideview mirror as we pulled away from Pratt, and he threw his hat, then punched a car. He shook his hand out and rested his head on top of the car in what was a spectacular rendition of being remorseful – but I wasn't buying it. I felt my happiness shred into confetti-sized pieces as I watched him disappear from my sight.

Pratt Montgomery is an asshole. He broke my heart before I even had the chance to offer it to him.

Chapter 10

When we made it home I threw my stuff on the kitchen table and ran upstairs to my room. I heard my mom ask what was the matter with me, and where Pratt was. When my brother began explaining what had happened, I slammed my bedroom door. *Yes, Princess was acting like a crybaby...and I didn't care.*

Truth be told, Pratt didn't technically do anything wrong. He was only guilty of douchebaggery in the first degree. We had hooked up, that's all. My biggest issue was how foolish I felt. I thought we had a pretty great connection, but it turned out the only connection between us was sex. And that's what pissed me off the most. If it was just a hook-up, why go through the charade of acting like you cared? Why hold my hand? Why pull me close to you and kiss my forehead? Why go through the motions, when I had already given it up to him?

I knew we weren't a couple, but what I hadn't banked on was him pulling something like that – and I certainly didn't expect to have this strong of a reaction. I'd be lying if I said I didn't really like him. Like, I had even looked past the holidays and contemplated if we could work something out long distance until we graduated, or something. *Welp, when you're wrong, you're so wrong.*

There was a knock at my door and my mom asked if she could come in.

"Sure," I said flatly.

She came in, holding a few baby wipes in her hand. "For your eye makeup," she explained, and handed them over.

"Thank you," I sniffled, and took one of the wipes. When I swiped my eye, I could feel all the gunkiness of the mascara rolling off. *This ought to be pretty.* I folded it in half and wiped again. Then I repeated it with a clean one again, on both eyes, until I felt like I had wiped away everything from my face. Including the pain. I didn't want to put my mom through any worry, especially at Christmas.

"Trent told us what happened. Want to talk about it?" She sat down next to me.

"What's there to talk about? I'm fine. We've spent a week and a half together, it's not like we were headed to Vegas for a 'Very Elvis Christmas Wedding'," I snorted, then blew my nose with one of the wipes.

"No, but you two looked pretty chummy...and adorable together," she said. "I guess that's why I'm so shocked. I saw how he watched you, and how he'd smile if you said something silly or did something London-esque. Even when you talked, he hung on every word. I just can't believe it."

"Well, believe it. Saw it with my own two peepers." I lay back on my bed and let out a loud exhale. "The pathetic part of all this is I hope he comes back if he has nobody to spend Christmas with. He needs to be around people who care. He hasn't had that in a while."

"I don't think Trent will agree to that. He's pretty pissed off," Mom informed me.

"I'll talk to him. Let me get changed." I hugged her.

"It just doesn't seem like something he'd do," she said. "He's always been such a stand-up kid. I guess my character judgment isn't as good as it used to be." She shrugged and stood up.

"I'll be right down."

I stood up too…and then we heard a bunch of thumps out in the hallway. I opened my door to see what it was, and caught my brother kicking Pratt's bags down the steps. Then he picked up Pratt's hockey stick and went to crack it over his knee, but I stopped him.

"Trent, don't do that. He didn't do anything wrong. We weren't in a committed relationship, for the love of all that is holy." My voice went up an octave and I clenched my hands in frustration.

Trent stared at me blankly, and then slowly kicked Pratt's duffle bag down the steps.

"I won't allow him to make a fool of you, London. I warned him beforehand that if he wasn't ready for anything, he shouldn't even look twice in your direction."

"If he comes here to get his stuff, he's welcome to stay. Do you understand, Trent? He has no family." I clenched my teeth and took a step towards him, so we were maybe a foot apart.

"Of course. Whatever Princess wants." He dropped the hockey stick, then bowed to me theatrically.

I tried to reason with him. "Trent, why are you so mad? He didn't do anything wrong." Convincing them was probably going to be a hell of a lot easier than convincing myself.

"Because, London, I told him this would happen. Once Alexi got bored or caught wind that he was seeing someone, she'd do this. Then when she had him hooked again on whatever it is that he sees in her, she'd dump him again. It's been an ongoing thing. She's always dangled herself in front of him, and at the first sign of happiness she'd cry she was sorry, then yank it out from under him. I can't help him anymore. I can't because after what he told me about you, about him believing that you were his one shot at true happiness…and he didn't even give it a real shot. He fucked up royally passing you up for that piece of trash."

He kicked the hockey stick, and it slid down the stairs. As I watched it go, all the events of the last few days started to make sense.

"Yeah, well. I wish he thought the same. But that's his choice." *If I said it out loud, I might start to believe it.*

"Alexi stopped by his aunt's thinking she'd find him there," Trent continued. "Then she and Hannah took a trip out here, once she knew where he was. She called and she texted him, relentlessly. He ignored her. I called her to tell her to leave him alone, and she said she wanted to hear it from him. He got on the phone and told her to leave him alone. Told her he was happy. When she saw you and Pratt at the mall together I knew, I *knew* she would try something, so I decided to go talk with her. Pratt stayed behind and out of sight, but he wanted to be there in case she got out of control. Because that's what she does. She's head case number two, Hannah's best friend."

He leaned against the wall and ran his hand through his hair. From the expression on his face he looked pretty stressed out still, but it seemed like he'd talked out some of his anger. My mom and I exchanged glances, then I hugged him.

"Thank you for worrying about me," I said. "But don't ruin your friendship with him over this. I'll be fine. Like I said, he didn't do anything wrong. The heart wants what the heart wants, and clearly he isn't over her – and that's okay. As long as he's happy, that's what counts. If things don't work out this time, hopefully for his sake he won't keep going back to her. So please, if he comes back here, just don't do anything drastic. Let it go. I'll be okay. I'm not saying I'll be a bucket of sunshine *but* I will be polite and I won't make things uncomfortable for anyone. Deal?" I stuck out my hand.

"You're too good for him, sis. But you got a deal." He took my hand and pulled me in for another hug.

Then Mom hugged us both, and announced that this was enough drama to last her a lifetime – she was going to bed.

Trent texted Pratt to let him know the front door was open and he was still welcome in our home, but he should just give me some space. Then he headed to bed himself. I was still a bit wired from the events of the evening and I really hadn't had much time to take it all in, so I decided to grab my Mac and head out to the barn. I went to find Tuna and bring him with me for company, but he was already asleep with Trent.

"Traitor," I whispered, and smiled as I closed the door to Trent's room.

I made some coffee and grabbed a blanket, then headed out there. Luckily I could control the thermostat from an app, so I had turned the heat up as my coffee was brewing, and it was nice and warm by the time I got there. *Some after party, eh London?*

I got settled in up in the loft, and put on some music. While I was plugging in the light strands I saw all the presents I had gotten for Pratt poking out from underneath the blanket I'd thrown over them. One of the barn cats must have been sleeping under there or something.

I plopped down on my comfy pillow bed, put on my headphones, and turned up the music. I started out checking my email. I hadn't set it up on my phone yet so I had a ton to go through from school, and friends wishing me a Merry Christmas and Happy New Year. Then I got to thinking, and I started snooping. First thing I did was Google Hannah because I knew her first and last names. Then when I found her Facebook page I looked through her friends for Alexi. And there she was, all five foot five inches of perky cute blond psycho…and I began to cry. I may not have been able to blame Pratt but I sure as hell was entitled to be upset. I really liked him, and I thought we had great chemistry. Turned out that wasn't enough. I still had the knot in my stomach that had formed earlier when I saw him kissing Alexi. Defending Pratt to my mom and brother was one thing. Actually getting over it was another.

I was lying on my side listening to some Taylor Swift when I felt a hand on my shoulder. I screamed and threw my headphones off my head. It was Pratt. I honestly did *not* expect to see him that night. I thought for sure I'd have some time to process what had happened, and be less angry by the morning if he was back at the house.

"Are you crazy?" I yelled at him. "You scared the shit out of me, Pratt. What are you even doing up here?"

"I'm sorry. I tried texting you but I got no response. When I got here I saw the lights on, and I wanted to talk to you." He sat next to me, but on the floor. I sat up, avoiding any eye contact with him.

"London, let me explain," he said. "Please?"

"No. I'm not really interested, Eighty-Six. You don't owe me an explanation – it's not like we were together or had planned on being together. Right? I mean, I was a holiday hook-up. That's cool. I just wish I had seen you kissing your ex-girlfriend before I gave it up to you. At least then I'd still have my dignity and I wouldn't feel like such a whore or a fucking fool for actually having feelings for you." I didn't look at him until the last few words of my sentence.

He got up on his knees and took my face in his hands. "Please. Just hear me out."

"Fine," I said with a shrug, fighting back the tears because I still wanted him, and I felt weak.

"I assume Trent told you about Alexi?" he asked.

"Actually, no, Hannah did – when she followed me out to taunt me about you kissing Alexi. Trent had to fill me in on the rest of the juicy tidbits on the ride home." I rolled my eyes and pulled away from his hands.

"I don't want to go backwards, London. Let me just tell you what happened tonight. Okay?" He pushed the hair away from my eyes, and I flinched a bit. Not in fear, in that 'get away from me' sense. Just because he *technically* didn't do anything wrong didn't mean I wasn't itching to punch him for doing what he did. Maybe I was hurt and feeling foolish for assuming he and I weren't just hooking up. Whatever the reason, I didn't want him to touch me. It reminded me that I was a dumbass.

He took my hand and tried to pull me to him.

"Pratt. This is fine. Just tell me so I can get back to my Cats of Instagram." I dismissed his advance for me to sit with him, and picked at the fringe on one of my pillows.

"London, I know, believe me I *know* what it looked like because I *was* kissing her, only to prove to her that I was *finished* with her."

"Yeah, okay." I snorted and picked up my headphones. "I was ready to listen until you fed me that line of bullshit, Eighty-Six. You can leave now and go to hell for trying to make me out to be some dumb bitch who'll buy anything you say."

"Stop. I swear it's the truth. She told me if I kissed her one last time she would leave me alone forever." He sounded desperate for me to hear him out.

"Ohhh, I see, and you believed her because she has such an upstanding character and truthfulness about her?" I stood up. I was getting pissed. *He really thinks I'm a special kind of stupid, doesn't he?*

"Don't say any more, please," I said. "I was cool with you sticking around for the rest of the break, but now that you've insulted my intelligence you can take your happy lying ass on the road. Maybe Alexi will have you stay with her until school gets back in." I raised my voice and walked over to the window with my arms folded. "I can't believe you expected me to just believe you. Just like that, right?"

I threw my hands up, infuriated by everything that was happening. I totally thought I had it under control – that I could be diplomatic about the entire situation – but I couldn't. I know it sounds dramatic, but I *really* liked him and I'd thought there could be more to us. It was a double whammy, to the heart and ego.

"I was hoping you would…but I suspected you wouldn't. So I did this." He came over and placed his phone in front of me on the sill. "I'll go get my stuff together and come back for my phone. Just hit play," he said as he walked off.

"Wait." I turned to him. "Take those with you." I pointed to the pile of presents from my mom and me. I didn't even know she had picked him up anything until we got back from the mall.

He gave a small smile and shook his head. "This is why I want to be with you London. You care. You make me happy. I haven't smiled the way I smile when I'm with you in a very long time. Long before my family's accident."

"I guess you should have thought of that before…" I began, but he interrupted me.

"I made a judgment call, and I can't apologize for it because I knew the only way I would get to be with you, in peace, happy, is if I made Alexi see it was over. *For good.* She knew that whole 'kiss me and tell me you don't love me' bullshit got me every single time. This time it bit her in the ass, because I told her the truth. No, I don't. Now leave me alone. I'm happy with London."

I had begun to tear up, and then the slippery little suckers started to fall out of my eyeballs. I hit play on his phone and heard him pretty much repeat everything he'd just said, word for word. He'd recorded the entire thing to prove to me that he wanted me.

After it ended I turned to him and wiped my tears.

"That doesn't make it right, Pratt. Seeing that *really* hurt me," I sniffled.

"Hurt me, too." He chuckled and looked at his hand, and I smacked his arm. "London, I'm sorry I hurt you, it wasn't what I set out…." he began, but I wrapped my arms around his neck and kissed him.

"I forgive you. I may not like it, it may feel like you sucker-punched me, but I understand, now." I laid my head on his chest. "Just don't do that shit again, Eighty-Six."

"So, are you saying you'll give me another chance?" He gave me dimple, and my insides turned to mush.

"I guess so. I mean it is the season of giving and all." I nudged him and gave a playful grin.

"I guess I should go talk to Trent," he said, looking out the window towards my house.

"He's asleep. Besides, you have some making up to do." I pulled him down with me onto the pillow bed.

"I sure do," he said, kissing my neck, and I laughed as he started tickling me.

"I love to hear you laugh, London. It makes me smile. I don't think I've ever been this happy. The last few days have shown me that life doesn't have to continue to be a sad road for me. There are still people who care. I got scared when I saw Alexi tonight, and I was so afraid I'd lose you." He searched my face as he spoke. "That I'd lose you before I even had the chance to love you."

"I think you have a pretty good chance of being stuck with me, Eighty-Six." I ran my hand down the side of his face.

"There's no other person I'd rather be stuck with, Princess," he said. And then he kissed me.

Other Books by HJ Harley

The Love Lies Bleeding Series

Finding Jordie Book One

Finding Nathan Book Two (February 2015)

Finding Rachel Book Three (June 2015)

18926089R00036